A Ghost-Light in the Attic

A Ghost-Light
in the Attic

Pat Thomson

Illustrated by Annabel Large

A & C Black · London

FLASHBACKS

Julie and the Queen of Tonga · Rachel Anderson
Across the Roman Wall · Theresa Breslin
The Doctor's Daughter · Norma Clarke
A Candle in the Dark · Adèle Geras
All the Gold in the World · Robert Leeson
The Saga of Aslak · Susan Price
Mission to Marathon · Geoffrey Trease

First paperback edition 1997
First published 1995 in hardback by
A & C Black (Publishers) Ltd
35 Bedford Row, London WC1R 4JH

Text copyright © 1995 Pat Thomson
Illustrations copyright © 1995 Annabel Large

ISBN 0-7136-4672-1

Photoset in Linotron Palatino by
Rowland Phototypesetting Ltd,
Bury St Edmunds, Suffolk

Printed in Great Britain by
St Edmundsbury Press Ltd,
Bury St Edmunds, Suffolk

Contents

· 1 ·

The Old Hall

'Is this the right place?' asked Tom. 'There's no one here.'

'There must be,' answered Bridget. 'Mum said she'd see us at Bridgeford Hall at four o'clock. You're right, though. It does look empty.'

'Dark and creepy,' said her brother.

Bridget looked up at the mullioned windows of the old house. It was large but not the huge, stately home she had been expecting. She opened the iron gate and stared down at the worn flagstone path. The doorstep had worn down, too. She realised that for hundreds of years, real people had worn that step down, coming and going. She walked slowly up to the heavy, wooden door. Real people had opened and closed it, their hands on that handle. Hesitantly, she knocked, then walked in.

The hallway was quite dark. A clock ticked loudly.

'Mum,' called Bridget.

'They're upstairs,' said Tom. Faint voices drifted down to them and they hurried up the staircase. All the doors at the top were shut.

'This one,' said Tom as the voices came again. He paused. Behind the door, one of the voices was whispering 'Hide him, hide him! Quickly!' Tom opened the door slowly. The room was empty.

Downstairs, there was the sound of footsteps, doors banging and shouts.

'Thank goodness,' said Bridget, 'someone's come,' and they turned and ran down the stairs again. The hall, however, was still empty.

Just then, a thin, high scream came from across the hall where a room led off into the shadows. They turned and dashed for the front door. At that moment, it was flung open and Mum came in, clutching a very ordinary plastic bag from the supermarket.

'There you are,' she said. 'Just been out for sandwiches. Did you meet Mr Wetherby?'

'Where is he?' asked Bridget. 'Is he in the house?'

'Oh, probably.' Mum said vaguely. 'I really need to stay on for a bit tonight. Ah, here you are,

Nick. You've got a job for these two, haven't you?'
A young man walked in. He had been working
outside. He shook hands.

'We're going to put you two in the attic to keep
you out of mischief,' he said, cheerfully.

'You don't mind, do you?' Mum didn't wait for
an answer but led the way to a back room where
she started to fill a kettle. Things seemed ordinary
again. 'I'm so excited! All this belongs to the
Historical Trust now and we can start work. Old
Mr Linton has left us everything and as he lived
abroad for most of his life, as his father did, the
house is a kind of time capsule. It's untouched, a
treasure house!' She handed out sandwiches and
cups of tea. 'This is Mr Wetherby, by the way,' she
said, remembering her manners. 'He says you can
work here during the holidays.'

'How kind,' murmured Tom, but Mum just
laughed.

'It's fascinating,' she said. 'You'll see.'

Mr Wetherby was looking at them. He seemed
amused. 'I can understand that you may be less
enthusiastic than your mother, but I would really
value your help. It's going to be an enormous task.
I'd like you to sort through some things in the old

nursery. Just unpack them carefully and line them up. Someone else will be working on them later but the sorting will save us hours. The nursery's in the attic. I'll show you when you're ready.'

The children's room was on the top floor. The door was low but wide. The latch was large and Bridget thought that a child would need both hands to lift it. She also noticed scratch marks at the bottom of the door. They were the kind of scratch marks made by a cat or a small dog.

'Do you mean we'll have to stay up here on our own?' asked Bridget.

'Don't worry,' laughed Mr Wetherby, 'we're only one floor down.' He opened the door with one hand and they walked into a big attic. Massive beams curved right down to the floor. Bridget went over to the window and looked down on the garden and the wood beyond.

'Look at this rocking horse,' said Tom and touched it gently, setting it rocking. There was also a large central table in the room, surrounded by piles of objects in all sorts of containers.

'It's a bit of a mess in here,' said Mr Wetherby. 'When things got a bit worn, I expect they were demoted to the nursery. Then it became a general storage area. The great thing is, hardly anything was ever thrown away.' He gave them a clipboard and a pencil and left them to get on with it.

'How do we start?' asked Tom.

'If Mr Wetherby had seen your bedroom he wouldn't have bothered,' said Bridget. She went over to the window again. 'It's strange. Lots of children must have stood here. They would have all been wearing different clothes from different ages but all of them must have stood here, like me.'

From the high window, she could see a path winding through the wood. It led to what looked like a gate in the boundary wall. As she looked at the gate, she felt afraid. She swallowed and stepped back from the window.

'What's up, Bridget?' Tom was staring at her. He looked startled.

'Nothing,' said Bridget. 'I don't know. I just felt funny.'

'You've gone all white. Was it what happened before? Did you hear the voices?'

Bridget seemed confused, then she turned to the shelves. 'Let's start by picking up all the smaller items and putting them up here,' she said, very briskly. 'Then we won't stand on them.'

There was a soft, slithering noise behind them. Whirling round, they saw that a sheet, which had been covering a large picture, had slipped to the floor. It was a family portrait. They stared at the family and the family stared back.

The man looked at them steadily, with dark, sad eyes. His hair was long but uncurled, his clothes brown. The lady at his side wore a long, black gown with a wide, white collar. Her closely fitting cap was trimmed with lace and she smiled a little. The older boy looked very like his father. They had the same dark eyes.

There were two small children, both wearing long skirts. One was holding a perch, a bird fluttering on it. The other sat on the table, a placid little soul it seemed, clutching something made of silver and coral. Bridget could not help smiling at the baby's round, cheerful face. Then she looked at the last child, a girl standing a little apart. The girl looked directly out at her, eye to eye, a half smile on her lively face. She was holding a lute.

'She looks fun,' said Tom. He was looking at the girl, too. 'If you got in her way, she'd crown you with that guitar.'

'Lute,' corrected Bridget. *'The Bassingbourn Family 1648,'* she read. 'It has their names on. *John and Philadelphia*. They're the parents.'

'Philadelphia!' grinned Tom.

'The girl is called Elinor. I like that. The big boy is Edmund. Oh!' she said, surprised, 'The one in a dress, the tiny one, he's a boy! He's called Nathaniel!'

'He must have felt really daft, wearing that.'

'I suppose it would have been the same for everyone. The one carrying the bird is Margaret. I think she's a little pet. You're right, though, Elinor looks the most interesting. I think the painter thought so, too. She seems so alive, almost speaking to him.'

'She's almost speaking to us, too. I bet that's her dog.'

Bridget looked. A small dog. About the right height to make those scratches. 'I think she used to be in this room a lot,' she said, slowly. 'I wonder if any of these things belonged to her?'

Suddenly, it all seemed much more interesting. They began to sort out the piles of objects, arranging them on the shelves and writing down the descriptions. There were some items which neither of them recognised.

'We need books,' said Tom, at last. 'Books to look things up. This is a serious job. It's stupid not to know the name of anything. Let's ask Mr Wetherby.'

'Right,' Bridget answered. 'Let's go now. No,

wait a moment. Look at this. It's the thing in the portrait.' In her hand, she held a little, silver stick, hung with bells. It had a whistle at one end, a piece of coral at the other. She shook it gently.

'It's the baby's rattle,' smiled Tom.

Bridget took it over to the portrait and compared it with the painting. 'It's the same one,' she said. 'You can see he's going to put that bit of coral in his mouth.' She put it down carefully in front of the portrait. 'Let's go and see Mr Wetherby now. I want to know more about this family.'

As the door closed behind them, the girl in the portrait smiled a little. But then, she had been smiling before.

Then, very gently, she ran her fingers over the strings of the lute.

· 2 ·

The Little Ghost

They found Mr Wetherby working on some papers. He waved to a pile of books and told them to help themselves.

'Mr Wetherby,' said Bridget, 'do you know who the Bassingbourns were?'

'You found the portrait, then.' He smiled and put his pencil down. 'It's delightful, isn't it? They lived here at the time of the Civil War. The family's greatest drama occurred then.'

'What happened?'

'I'm working on that. I would guess it was a family row. The eldest son, Edmund, seems to have left the family home completely.'

'He must have fought on the wrong side during the war,' decided Tom.

'That's the obvious answer,' nodded Mr Wetherby, 'but although there's no trace of him after the war, I came across just one letter from him to the family. Very warm and loving. It doesn't fit in with the theory of a split, does it? A bit of a mystery there.'

'Take a torch when you go back up,' called Mum from the next room. 'There's no electricity on the top floor. Be careful of the stairs.'

They scampered up the first flight of stairs. Tom stopped to slide on the wide floorboards of the landing. Bridget waited for him at the foot of the next flight.

'It's getting a bit dark,' she said.

They stopped talking and their clattering feet sounded very loud. They stepped more quietly in the soft, evening light. Tom was listening to something, his face screwed up.

'Thought I heard music,' said Tom. 'Can't be, unless the others have some tapes with them.' He started up the last steps.

'Stop,' whispered Bridget. 'Can you hear that little noise? Like a dog scratching?'

'Birds in the roof,' said Tom and walked into the attic.

Bridget followed slowly, reluctantly. Nothing seemed changed. Fading light fell across the table. They stood in silence for a moment.

'Tom,' said Bridget, 'you don't believe, do you? In ghosts, I mean?'

'No,' said Tom, firmly. 'There's always funny noises in old houses. Anyway,' he continued, going over to the picture, 'they look a nice crowd.' He gave a thumbs-up sign to the girl. 'There. She's smiling. It's O.K.' He grinned cheerfully at Bridget but she did not respond.

She became very busy, sorting out the objects. She held each one up and Tom found the description and read it out.

'*A blackjack,*' he read, '*a leather drinking mug.*' He giggled. 'It says the French thought Englishmen drank out of their boots because of these!'

'The rattle!' said Bridget.

'So? One baby's rattle.'

'It's here on the shelf again. We put it over by the portrait.'

Tom looked over to the portrait. 'You're right. But it can't have moved.'

'Something *is* happening, Tom. It's no good! There *is* something strange about this room!'

Then the noises started. The rocking horse began to rock. The bells of the rattle tinkled. A scratching sound came from the door and when they ran to look, they saw the scratches forming on the door, scored by invisible claws. They both jumped as a low chuckle sounded very close by.

Tom was ready to run but, to his astonishment, Bridget stepped right into the centre of the room. She was angry.

'Stop it!' she shouted. 'I'm not afraid. Just stop it at once!'

Someone spoke.

'What a passion you are in!'

Bridget and Tom looked towards the portrait. There were two girls and two lutes. A girl in the picture and a girl standing in front of it. They stared as she turned and put her lute back into the picture. The painted instrument absorbed its twin. Tom and Bridget found they were hanging on to each other, but the girl smiled.

'You wanted to meet me, did you not? You looked on me very favourably, I thought.'

Bridget's throat seemed to have dried up but she managed an answer. 'We are very pleased to meet you.' She felt she ought to speak very properly.

Tom found his voice. 'You must be Elinor Bassingbourn.'

The girl curtsied. 'This room is much changed,' she complained. 'I never know how it will be when I come up.' She set the horse rocking. 'This is not ours. It belongs to the shadow children.'

'Are they here, too?' Tom asked, nervously.

'Who knows?' Elinor shrugged. 'We are sad and tedious in this house. These are troubled times. I shall stay with you awhile. Oh, you have found my brother's trunk.' She ran over to a small leather trunk. 'This is Mun's. Look. "E.B." Edmund Bassingbourn. He is too old to care for these things now so I play with them. He travels abroad at this moment.' She sighed. 'I miss him.'

She opened the lid and took out a top and whip. Tom came over and started to finger the objects.

'Clay marbles,' he said, spilling them out of the bag. 'And what are these?'

'Knucklebones,' said Elinor and threw them in the air, catching them on the back of her hand.

'Fivestones!' said Tom, recognising the game. 'These really are bones, aren't they?'

'From a mutton stew, without doubt. Ah,' she said, diving into the trunk again, 'this ball is Pepper's favourite. Come, Pepper.'

Bridget saw a white blur, heard claws rattle along the floorboards and then saw a small dog leaping excitedly around Elinor. It was the dog from the portrait. 'So he *was* there,' said Bridget. 'He was scratching at the door.'

'It puts Master Bragshaw in a rage. He would have Pepper kept in the stables. I hate him.'

'Who's Master Bragshaw?' asked Tom.

'The steward. When father is from home, he is quite horrid. He is clever and suspicious. You must be careful when you come and visit me.'

'Shall we come and visit you, then?'

'Oh yes,' said Elinor, serenely. 'Oh look, Mun's soldiers. His miniature army.' She set up a row of them. 'My mind runs on soldiers at the present. There are too many of them abroad in the countryside, Grandmother says. I fear something disagreeable is going to happen.'

'Is there a war, then?' asked Tom.

'Father would protect us but he keeps going away.'

Bridget looked at the girl. She was quite young, really, and almost ready to cry. 'Don't worry, Elinor,' she said and, very hesitantly, took her hand. It was soft and warm and the little face soon became lively again.

'I shall think of other things.' She picked up the rattle. 'This is Nat's. Let us make a visit now. Come along. Down the long staircase.'

Elinor's hand was resting against the wall of the alcove but now they saw a latch under her fingers. The blank wall was fading. Instead, they saw the solid, wide planks of a door and Tom realised that the alcove had once been a doorway. He felt excited but apprehensive, too. On the other side was Elinor's world.

The little girl opened the door. A flight of steps led down into the darkness. Tom backed away and looked across at Bridget. At that moment, Pepper dashed through the doorway and Bridget, as if in a dream, walked straight through after him.

'Bridget!' whispered Tom.

'Come,' said Elinor, impatiently.

Tom breathed in deeply as if he were about to dive underwater and followed his sister. He heard the latch click as Elinor closed the door on their century and took them into her own.

· 3 ·

Invisible

They were walking down a narrow, wooden staircase. Tom listened to the click of Elinor's shoes on the treads but his own and Bridget's made no sound. At the turn of the stairs they passed a low door, then sounds from below began to reach them. He heard distant voices, a clattering of pots and then, quite near, the ticking of a clock. They were entering a stone-flagged hall. He looked at the clock which only had one hand. Here, it was the middle of the afternoon.

'Bridget,' whispered Tom, 'what have we done? Will we be able to get back?'

'Don't worry,' said Bridget. She still seemed dreamy. 'We can go back to the attic.'

They followed Elinor across the square hall. Bridget recognised the front door and realised they were on the ground floor. Elinor walked straight into a room which led off the hall and Bridget and Tom followed, very warily. No one seemed to notice them at all. They slipped behind a high-backed chair, just inside the door.

Elinor curtsied. A woman was lying on a long cane chair, a kind of day bed. She smiled at Elinor but an older woman, seated at a gate-legged table, turned and spoke sharply to her.

'Where have you been, Elinor? I have been waiting to give you your writing lesson.'

'I have been practising my lute, Grandmother,' said Elinor, smoothly.

'She plays well, now,' said the younger woman.

Grandmother snorted. 'You indulge your daughter too much, Philadelphia. No good will come of it.'

There were also two small children in the room. The youngest one was holding the rattle and put the coral in his mouth.

'Nat is breeding his teeth,' Elinor said knowledgeably. 'The coral comforts him.'

Her mother sighed. 'You are right, Elinor,' she said. 'Nurse says he is much troubled by them. Little Margaret, however, is as good as gold.'

Margaret seemed to be about four or five. She was playing quietly with her wooden doll.

Bridget, peeping over the back of the chair, noticed that the doll was also dressed in a long gown with a broad collar and a little cap, just like her owner. The little girl looked up, straight at Bridget, but gave no sign of having seen her.

'They can't see us,' whispered Bridget.

'They can't hear us, either,' replied Tom but he whispered too.

There was a noise in the yard. Hooves clattered and voices called.

'The wagon! Ned and Bragshaw must have returned,' cried Elinor and ran to the window.

'It will be the new carpet, Philadelphia,' said Grandmother and the ladies rose in some excitement and hurried past Tom and Bridget into the hall.

Bridget looked around. There were certainly no carpets in the room. Everything seemed to be made of polished wood and there was very little furniture.

'Bragshaw brings us the carpet,' whispered Elinor to Bridget and Tom. 'Stay behind the chair.'

The carpet was brought in and put on the table. A young servant spread it out under Bragshaw's direction. 'I congratulate you,

Madam,' he said. 'An excellent choice.' He smoothed down his hair and clasped his bony hands.

'Thank you, Bragshaw,' said Philadelphia, rather shortly, Bridget thought. But the steward was looking at Grandmother, intending to please her.

'You will be the first in the neighbourhood, yet again, Mistress Bassingbourn. No one else has such a fine carpet.'

'It is our duty to move with the times,' said Grandmother, piously. 'In London I hear that they spread carpets on the floor. That does not seem reasonable to me. They would wear out in no time. Put it in the court cupboard, Ned,' she said to the young serving man. 'We shall keep it there.'

'What news do you bring from town?' Philadelphia interrupted.

'There has been a battle, Madam, at Worcester. There are soldiers everywhere.'

Bridget saw an immediate change in the old lady's face. She looked afraid.

'The enemy was soundly beaten,' continued Bragshaw. 'There will be no king again in this country. Our brave men pursue the last of the Royalist rabble.'

'Sad times, nevertheless,' said Philadelphia, 'when men fight. Thank you, Bragshaw, we are pleased with the carpet.' She nodded and he left the room at last. As soon as the door shut, Philadelphia spoke again. 'You must not worry, Madam. John Bassingbourn's name is respected. It is well known that your son is a loyal Parliamentarian.'

'I do not fear for myself. I fear for our young hothead. It is also well known that Edmund has defied his father.' She sighed. 'Will these troubles never end?'

Elinor slipped from the room and Bridget and Tom followed. Elinor crossed the hall cautiously and led them up the staircase again to the low door they had passed on their way down. Inside there was a tiny room, with a tiny window. Bridget felt the solid wooden floor under her feet but could only see dimly. Elinor fumbled in the gloom and then struck a spark.

'I will light the nip,' she said.

A smell which reminded Bridget of old chip fat filled the little room. Elinor was holding a little tin box, filled with smouldering straw. She had used it to light a kind of long taper, made from a rush.

Then she put a round tin back into the drawer of a small table. Bridget noticed the carved drawer handle was in the shape of the head of a cherub. There was very little else in the room and they sat on the floor. She could see a trunk, shaped out of a hollow log and covered with animal hide with the hair still on. There was a wooden doll like Margaret's on the floor.

'That was a tinder box you used,' Tom was saying, quite shocked. 'You could burn the house down. Does your mother know you have it?'

'Let us not talk of what is known or not known,' replied Elinor, rather grandly. 'We came here to talk of Bragshaw. I do not trust him. He does not like Ned and me because we have caught him listening at doors. That makes him very angry.' She beamed at the idea of making Bragshaw angry.

'Elinor,' said Tom, suddenly, 'what are these sad times everyone is speaking of?'

Elinor looked very serious. 'It is because King Charles had his head cut off.' Her eyes grew round at the thought. 'But his son returns with an army and now all is confusion again. There has been a battle at Worcester and the King's son and all his poor men must fly for their lives. Grandmother cried when the King was executed but father said it must be so for the sake of the country. Father does not always agree with Grandmother on these matters. Nor did Mun agree with father. My brother loved the King and wanted to serve in his son's army. That is why he went away.'

Her face crumpled and she picked up her doll.

'Don't worry,' said Bridget. 'At least Mun will be safe if he's away.'

'Ned thinks we shall have a message from Mun soon,' whispered Elinor, 'but he doesn't want Bragshaw to learn of it. Could you watch him? To see if he means any evil to Mun?'

The light was burning down and Tom looked at it nervously.

'I don't know how much we can help,' said Bridget, 'but we will try.' She held Elinor's small hand. 'How shall we come to you?'

'You will come if I need you. That is how it is.'

The flame died as Elinor spoke. Bridget found she was holding the wooden doll and the floor felt hard and cold.

A light showed in the doorway but it was not

the low door of Elinor's secret room. It was the door of the attic and Mr Wetherby was coming to fetch them with a torch.

'What devotion to duty!' he said. He seemed to be bellowing. 'Oh, I say! That's a find!' He took the doll out of Bridget's hands. 'I didn't see that before. I'll have a proper look at it tomorrow. Now be careful on the stairs. It's pretty dark.'

Mum was already waiting in the hall, jangling her car keys. 'All right to come back tomorrow?' she asked. 'It's not too tedious, is it?'

'Don't worry, Mum,' said Tom, 'we're coping. We don't mind helping.'

They went out of the front door, over the worn step. Mr Wetherby put out the ground floor lights one by one until all was darkness. Then, he came out, too, shut the front door and turned the key in the lock as they called good night. As they drove behind his car down the lane, Bridget touched Tom on the arm and pointed. He turned his head to look back. In the attic, a very small light showed. It was not the steady beam of a torch. It was the pale flickering of a rushlight.

· 4 ·

Spies

When Mum looked in the refrigerator the next morning and found it empty, she decided she would have to stop off at the supermarket on the way to Bridgeford Hall. So Tom and Bridget cycled over. They found Mr Wetherby in the barn and he waved them into the house.

'He must trust us,' said Tom, as they shut the attic door behind them. 'Let's get down to some work straight away.'

'I think Elinor must have her doll back,' said Bridget. She picked up the wooden doll and offered it to the girl in the portrait. Nothing happened. She felt slightly silly and put the doll down in front of the portrait. 'Do you think anything is going to happen?' she asked. 'Did it really happen yesterday? Can it happen again?'

'We can only wait and see,' answered Tom. 'Let's empty those boxes over there.'

It was mostly clothing in the boxes. In one she found little caps and gloves, some beautifully embroidered. Bridget looked in the next box and took out a Victorian bonnet, trimmed with artificial flowers.

'These must have been sorted out already,' she decided. 'Let's concentrate on the box from Elinor's time.' She plunged her hand into the soft fabric and felt something hard. It was a small shoe, square-toed, open at the side, with a faded rose fastening the front. Bridget wondered if it could have been Elinor's and as she thought of her, she heard music again. This time it was not the lute but a child, singing softly. They both froze. They could hear footsteps coming nearer and nearer on the other side of the blank alcove wall.

They heard the noise of the latch being lifted. Then, the blank wall dissolved into the door and Elinor came through it.

'Forgive me,' she said in a very grown-up manner. 'I disturb your researches but this day, Bragshaw goes into town and we are to go with him.'

'We?' asked Tom.

'Yes,' said Elinor as if it were quite natural. 'You are to watch Bragshaw. Ned takes the cart to bring home the new chest of drawers.' She obviously thought they would never have seen such an object. 'Mother says the old chests are inconvenient and it is quite the fashion to have these new sets of drawers. It is to be in walnut and very pretty.'

'Are we to go in the cart then?'

'Yes, it will be well packed with straw. I am to drive with Ned while my mother rides pillion with Bragshaw. We will meet in town at my Aunt Ferrer's house.'

This time, they followed her unhesitatingly through the door and down the stairs.

They were relieved to see Bragshaw already riding off with Mistress Bassingbourn seated behind him on the same horse. The cart was to follow behind and they were soon grateful that it was well padded with straw. The roads were full of pot holes and Bridget bit her tongue at one bump. She cried out before she could stop herself but Ned gave no sign of having heard her. The path ran through woodland and when they emerged, the town was within sight. Tom realised that it was, in fact, quite near. Having travelled a few miles over such roads, he understood why visits might not be frequent. He was sure he was bruised all over. As they entered the town, the cart shuddered over cobbles until Tom's teeth rattled.

They turned into a coach yard and came to a halt. Bragshaw had already gone inside the house and while Ned settled the horses, they hung around, watching the door. When Bragshaw emerged, Bridget and Tom slipped behind him and, keeping their distance, began to follow him down the street.

At the crossroads, there was a market hall. Under the high roof, they saw wool and yarns changing hands. In the open, people were offering their own produce. As they looked, Bragshaw glanced behind him. Then he started to thread his way through the stalls. 'Quick,' said Tom, 'don't lose him.'

They saw him move swiftly, turning often to look behind him, then slip down a narrow alley. They followed. The way was narrow, the houses almost meeting overhead. Then they turned a corner and saw Bragshaw was making for an ale house.

'No one except Elinor seems to be able to see us. Dare we go in?' asked Tom.

'Let's go round the back,' answered Bridget, pointing to a passageway.

The passage led to a dingy court. Most of the windows which gave on to the court were open.

'I'd keep these windows closed,' whispered Tom, holding his nose as he looked.

'Here,' hissed Bridget. 'He's here.'

They peered through the window and saw Bragshaw, so near that they drew back. He was sitting with a soldier and drinks were being brought to them. There were several other soldiers, all looking tired and bored, including one who looked too young to be in the army. They all wore jerkins made of buff leather and across their chests were leather straps with little metal cases hanging from them. Tom guessed that they might hold gunpowder. Some of the men wore round metal helmets but the others had quite ordinary hats. Bragshaw was talking in a low voice to the officer.

'It is certain that he was at Worcester and has not escaped to France,' he was telling the officer. 'Edmund Bassingbourn will be with the group of Royalists which is roaming the countryside.'

'But is young Charles with them?' demanded the officer.

'I am not certain,' Bragshaw admitted, 'but it is possible. The old woman would give the prince shelter.'

'John Bassingbourn serves Cromwell like us,' objected an older man. 'He is loyal.'

'But the old woman is not,' spat Bragshaw. 'She is a Catholic and a Royalist. And so is the fine Edmund.'

'Very well. We will watch the countryside around the house. When he approaches, we will send word. Set a trap for him and we will spring it.'

Although he had never met Edmund, Tom felt indignant.

'You will be well rewarded,' added the officer. 'Captain Eyre takes great pleasure in the hunt.'

'I shall gratefully accept any reward due,' said Bragshaw, 'but I do not do this for money.' He gazed at the ceiling. 'I do it for the sake of my conscience.'

Tom was very angry. He wished he could do something. Bridget sensed it and touched his arm.

'Are you suspected?' asked the officer.

'Master Bassingbourn trusts me absolutely,' replied Bragshaw, smugly.

Tom could bear it no longer. He moved closer to the window, and, leaning over the window sill and into the room, he stretched out his arm, putting his fingers just under the back of Bragshaw's hat-brim. Delicately, he began to tip it forward.

Bragshaw continued to talk and pushed the hat back, hardly noticing. Tom did it again. Bridget saw that the eyes of the other soldiers were fixed on Bragshaw. They were fascinated. When the hat fell forward for the third time, the young boy gave a little snort of laughter. The older man gave him a friendly cuff but he was grinning, too. When it happened again, they all began to laugh.

Bragshaw stiffened and turned towards the window. Tom and Bridget moved backwards quickly but Bragshaw only saw the empty court. His face was very red. They heard the officer speak, rather impatiently.

'There is no one outside the window. Your hat is ill-fitting, Sir. It can easily be adjusted.' Then he added, 'Or perhaps your head will grow to fit it.'

As they tiptoed away, they heard the boy. He had given way completely and was whooping with laughter.

The return journey was even more uncomfortable, squashed beside the fine new chest of drawers.

In the safety of the attic, Elinor received their news gravely. She curtsied and thanked them. 'Poor brother Edmund,' she said. 'My good Ned shall know of this. He will help me.' Then she stood in front of the portrait. 'We shall meet again before long. The time is drawing nearer,' and Elinor stepped into the portrait.

In a second, it was just a picture of a young girl from long ago, holding a painted lute.

· 5 ·

Two Traps

Tom and Bridget could not wait to get to the Hall the next morning. Their mother was surprised at their enthusiasm but relieved that they were not bored.

Mr Wetherby was upstairs, standing in front of the portrait when they arrived.

'Morning, Bassingbourns,' said Tom.

'A respectful bow wouldn't come amiss,' suggested Mum.

'Nothing elaborate,' warned Mr Wetherby. 'This was a solid, provincial, Parliamentarian family. Well, at least, John was. His mother was a Catholic.'

'Could you have Royalists and Roundheads in the same family?' asked Bridget.

'That was one of the sad things about the Civil War,' said Mr Wetherby. 'About any civil war, I suppose. Families were torn apart. The elder son, Edmund, was his Grandmother's favourite and I suspect he was a Royalist, as she was.'

'Of course,' said Bridget, 'that might be why he went away.'

'John Bassingbourn was a respected local man. I know that from the papers I've seen from other families. His sympathies were with Cromwell. His mother was probably tolerated for his sake. She was an old lady, after all.'

'So what happened after the Battle of Worcester?' asked Tom. 'The Roundheads won, didn't they?'

'Yes, the last great battle. The prince escaped. He lived to become Charles the Second.'

'But what about Edmund Bassingbourn?' asked Bridget.

'Sorry. No idea, yet. I'm still hoping to find more documents in the house. Still, can't be helped. Can you sort through these kitchen things today?' He held up a three-legged pan with a handle. 'This is a skillet.' He put it down in front of the portrait. 'You'll find stuff like this in that wooden crate.'

'That should keep them busy,' said Mum. 'Let's leave them to it.'

Tom sighed and fetched the reference books.

Bridget made a start. 'This is a spoon,' she pronounced.

'Thank you, O Brilliant One,' said Tom. 'Try something a little more difficult. What on earth's that?' He picked up a rectangular box with a piece of wood sticking up, like a mast. A piece of string ran up the mast, holding up a heavy block of wood. Foolishly, he plucked at the string. The block of wood dropped with such a fierce bang that he yelped. 'It's a trap!'

Bridget flicked through the pages of the reference book in a very professional way. 'So it is,' she said, calmly. 'It's called a *deadfall mousetrap*.'

'And I know why. It killed my finger!'

Bridget smiled but someone else laughed out loud. The girl in the portrait still held the lute but the girl in front of it held the skillet.

'Are you so grand,' asked Elinor, 'that you have never been in a kitchen and have to search in books? Come with me and I will show you these things. I know all the names you seek.'

'You would,' said Tom, sucking his finger.

'I also have something important to tell you.' They followed her boldly through the alcove door but she stopped on the stairs and turned to face them. 'I need you,' she said simply. 'Ned has news of my brother but he works in the kitchen at present for our good Woodthorpe. Soon, she will go to supervise the maids. Then, Ned will tell me what he knows.'

They crossed the flagstoned hall and went down two steps into a big kitchen where everyone was busy. No one even looked in their direction.

A large table dominated the centre of the room, just as a huge fireplace dominated the end wall. There was an open fire with a pot suspended over it. A girl was chopping herbs at the table and an older woman was plucking a goose, carefully collecting the feathers in a basket. They were both listening to Ned. He was mending a tangle of cogs and pulleys which hung above the fire. Tom recognised it as a spit. Ned's mind, however, was on his story.

'What did Master Saltmarsh find, then?' asked the older woman.

'A stranger, Mistress Woodthorpe, securely bound to a tree.'

The girl screamed and put down her knife. 'What? In our woods? Close to here?'

'In our woods,' repeated Ned, pleased with the effect. 'Two cut-throats had come at him, their pistols at the ready.'

'Were they going to cut his throat with their pistols?' enquired Mistress Woodthorpe.

Ned ignored her and spoke to the girl. 'He said they sprang at him from behind the hedgerow and pulled him from his horse.'

'I shall bide at home at night,' declared the girl. 'There are too many lawless soldiers on the roads.'

'I'll look after you, Peg,' offered Ned, at which the woman chuckled but Peg said it was a kind thought and she was much obliged.

'We must stir about,' said Mistress Wood-thorpe, 'the master will be back tomorrow.'

'Tomorrow?' Ned looked up, quickly. 'Tomorrow night?'

'Most likely – and we have much to do. Come, Peg, we must set those maids to work.'

As soon as the two women had gone, Elinor ran forward. 'Is it safe to talk now, Ned? Have you heard from Mun?'

The young man shook his head. 'But I've heard from a friend of his. Your brother is not far away.'

'Then it is true. He is not safely in France.'

'No.' Ned's face was serious now. 'It is as we feared. He returned to fight at Worcester.' He patted Pepper awkwardly. 'He will be a hunted man now. Cromwell's soldiers will be waiting for him.'

Elinor was holding Pepper so tightly, he started to struggle.

'His friend will bring news of him to the gate in the boundary wall. Bragshaw watches me closely. Can you go, Mistress Elinor and find out what the news is? I know you are but young . . .'

'I am old enough to help my brother,' said Elinor proudly.

'I will watch Bragshaw as he watches me. I will make sure you are not discovered.'

'Send to me secretly when it is time to go to the gate, then,' and Elinor left the kitchen, her head held high. At the foot of the stairs, however, she turned to Bridget and Tom. 'Will you come with me to the gate?' she asked, her small face anxious. 'If not, I must go alone even if he does not come until dark.' They both nodded. Elinor plunged into the folds of her skirts and brought out a large key which she had tied round her waist. 'Put this before the portrait and you will find me. You will know when it is time.'

'Mistress Elinor,' said a voice, 'to whom do you speak?'

Elinor froze. Bragshaw stood in the parlour doorway. He moved towards Elinor and as he took hold of her arm, Bridget and Tom slipped behind him.

'Have you heard from your brother, Edmund?' asked Bragshaw, shaking Elinor slightly.

'I believe there have been no letters for some time.'

'In your father's absence, I protect this household. You should confide in me.' Bragshaw towered over Elinor. Then he released her, put his hands behind his back and stood up straight. 'He would not approve of deceit or lies.'

Tom made a face behind Bragshaw's back to encourage Elinor but she also stood up very straight. Then Tom noticed a paper tucked into a tiny buttoned pocket on the man's sleeve. The button was undone. Tom stretched out his hand.

'I am sure,' said Elinor, stiffly, 'you cannot mean that I would seek to deceive you.' Tom's fingers closed on the paper. 'There would be no need,' she continued haughtily. 'If there was something I did not want you to know, I would not tell you.'

Tom heard Bragshaw's breath hiss and as the man raised his hand to strike Elinor, Tom found himself holding the paper. Elinor flinched but stood her ground. Bragshaw's hand dropped suddenly before he touched her. Tom stepped back quickly, treading on Bridget's feet.

'Run for it,' he said. 'Get back to the attic. I've got something important.' As he ran up the stairs, he dared only glance at the paper. He could just see the last line.

'Set the trap,' it said.

· 6 ·

Bad News

The door at the top of the stairs stood open but even as Tom closed it, it dissolved. He found his hand pressed against the flat wall. In his other hand, he held a piece of paper.

'You've done it now,' said Bridget. 'What if Elinor is blamed?'

'I think she can look after herself,' answered Tom, 'and she would definitely want to see this. Let's have a look.' He read it carefully. It was not easy, judging by his face. 'It's all "f"s,' he complained.

'That's a long "s",' Bridget explained. 'Let me see.' She made an angry noise. 'Elinor's right! Bragshaw *is* trying to catch Edmund. It's from those soldiers we saw in the ale house.'

Tom looked again. 'Bragshaw is working as a spy for the Roundheads. It's because there's a reward for catching Royalists, I bet.' He started to read aloud.

'The matter of which we spoke comes fast to its close. Expect the arrival soon of the party known to you. I lodge at The Civett Cat so send to me as soon as you have set the trap.'

'That's it, then,' said Bridget. 'They know that Edmund or his friend will try and contact someone here, and as soon as Edmund arrives, Bragshaw will let the soldiers know. We must get to Edmund's friend first.'

'We'd better try Elinor's key,' said Tom. 'Quickly.'

They put the key in front of the portrait and went to the alcove and looked hopefully at the blank wall. Something happened almost at once. Slowly, a door appeared but it looked different, more massive and battered, with an enormous lock. The key was in the lock. Tom turned it.

They found themselves in a garden. The sun was high and warm. A blackbird was noisy nearby. Immediately in front of them was a formal garden. It looked like a board game. Neatly arranged circles and shapes were formed by closely clipped box hedges which only came up to their knees. Each circle had a round box tree, like a lollipop, at its centre.

Bridget looked at the house. Tom touched her arm and pointed to a window. The casements were open and voices came floating quietly out into the garden. They moved a little closer.

It must have been the midday meal. Grandmother and Philadelphia were seated at the table with Elinor. The remains of a large fish were being carried out and on the table was what looked like a joint of roasted meat, some kind of game and a tart. They obviously did not go hungry. Grandmother was ordering Ned to pour the ale and they were slightly shocked to see Elinor had some, too.

'My discussions with William Lawson this morning were vastly satisfactory,' said Grandmother, looking pleased with herself. 'The garden is to be planned anew.'

'You will keep the Knot Garden, I hope?' asked Philadelphia.

Grandmother nodded. 'Certainly, my dear, but beyond the wall, all is to be both pleasant and useful. There will be a kitchen garden and an orchard on either side of a nut alley. Cherries, mulberries and medlars, I think. Yes, they will be a good addition to our resources.'

Elinor, who was tucking in and ignoring her

elders chose this moment to drop her bombshell. 'Master Saltmarsh told me yesterday that he has a fork.'

There was silence.

'What are you saying, child?' asked Grandmother.

'A fork. He is going to bring it to show you.'

Bridget and Tom were as surprised at the announcement as Grandmother but for different reasons. The effect was as if Elinor had said that Master Saltmarsh had a monkey up a stick. They looked at the table more closely. There were knives but no forks and they realised even the grown-ups had been eating with their fingers and pieces of bread.

'His son is lately returned from Italy,' offered Philadelphia. 'Perhaps he brought it from there.'

Grandmother tutted but was obviously intrigued. 'What nonsense!' she said. 'What does it look like?'

'An elegant bone handle and two prongs. It is little brother to the great pitchfork the cowman uses to clean . . .'

'Thank you, Elinor,' interrupted Philadelphia hastily. 'Take from the dish of colewort, then you may carry some cherry tart into the garden.'

Elinor ate a tiny amount of what was obviously cabbage and then took a large amount of cherry tart and made her escape into the garden. They heard the latch of the house door click and there was Elinor, gazing at them, tart halfway to her mouth.

'This way,' she said, and led them through a gate in the wall into the sheltered herb garden. Bridget could smell the lavender and hear the bees as they waited for Elinor to read Bragshaw's note.

'We were right,' she said calmly. 'Mun knew he was not to be trusted. He sets a trap for my brother.'

'Go to the boundary gate now,' said Bridget, 'then you can speak to your brother's friend the moment he arrives. Edmund must be warned not to come here.'

'You go with her,' said Tom. 'I'll keep watch and if Bragshaw should come this way, I can warn you.'

Bridget followed Elinor out of the garden, across the orchard and through the wood. 'We shall go quite boldly,' said Elinor. 'There is no reason why we should not be here.' Nevertheless, their pace slackened as they approached the gate.

Elinor opened the gate and looked out. Bridget recognised the lane that ran by the boundary wall but there was no hard surface now. It was muddy and deeply rutted. There was no one in sight and the woods which continued on the other side of the lane were silent. They closed the gate and came back to sit under a tree. Elinor pulled at the grass and Bridget did not know what to say to her. The noise of the falling leaves seemed unnaturally loud. Suddenly she knew that it was not the wind in the branches she could hear.

Instead, there was a flurry of leaves in the tree above them and a man dropped to the ground.

Elinor and Bridget sprang up but the man spoke.

'Elinor?'

She nodded.

'I thank God for that. Your brother said I could trust little Elinor. I expected to be in the tree all day!' He smiled and gave an elaborate bow. He was young, richly dressed but filthy. There was even mud on his face. One of his high boots was slashed. His cloak hung from one shoulder, revealing what had once been a white, lace-trimmed collar and frilled cuffs. They were now grey and torn.

'I have news for you,' he began.

Elinor interrupted him. 'Mun must not come. Someone is watching the house. He must leave this neighbourhood immediately. Look at this.' She handed him Bragshaw's note.

As he read it, he looked angry but also anxious. 'It is too late,' he said. 'Edmund must be brought here. We cannot take him further without risking his life. I must tell you he is injured. He was wounded in the battle.'

Terror in the Kitchen

Bridget had to admire Elinor. She looked like a small adult and now she behaved like one. Her face briefly showed shock, then she answered the young man. 'In that case, you must bring him here as soon as possible. But keep to the woods.'

'It will be done within the hour. My horse is hidden in the woodland across the lane. The rest of us must travel on tonight.'

'I will make the necessary arrangements to take him secretly to the house.'

'Are you sure, little one?' asked the man, kindly.

'Of course,' and Elinor bowed slightly.

Edmund's friend smiled and also bowed in return. Elinor opened the gate and looked out. She signalled to the man who fetched his horse and left swiftly, disappearing into the woods.

They found Tom running to meet them. 'Bragshaw's got a visitor. He told Ned not to disturb him for an hour.'

'Then I must talk to Ned.' Elinor picked up her skirts and ran, too.

Ned was in the stable. He looked so appalled when he was told of Edmund's injuries that Bridget wondered if they had been friends. They were about the same age, she guessed.

'There is nothing else to be done, Mistress Elinor, we must tell the ladies.'

Elinor looked doubtful but allowed Ned to lead the way to the parlour. Philadelphia was embroidering but Grandmother was standing by the window, looking out on the Knot Garden.

'What is it, Ned?'

Elinor shut the door and Ned spoke softly. 'It is Master Edmund, Madam.'

Grandmother turned, sharply. 'Edmund? News of Edmund?'

'He was injured in the battle, Madam.'

Philadelphia jumped up, bewildered. 'What battle? Edmund travels abroad!'

Grandmother sighed. 'Forgive me, my dear. Edmund returned to England. He was determined to fight for the future King. I begged him to remain in safety but he would not. I dared not speak of it.'

'Where is he now? How is he? His father will be so angry!'

'His friends are bringing him to the house, Madam,' continued Ned, quietly, 'but there are more troubles.'

'Bragshaw is a foul monster,' Elinor broke in. 'He wishes us ill.'

'Hush Elinor,' said Philadelphia, distractedly.

'It is true, Madam,' Ned confirmed. 'Show the paper.'

Philadelphia cried out in distress as she read. She could not believe that Bragshaw would do such a thing. She passed the note to Grandmother who waved it away. She seemed very weary.

'Edmund and I had our suspicions,' she said and sank into a chair.

Philadelphia began to weep but Grandmother was thinking. 'We must prevent Bragshaw from finding out that Edmund is actually here. We must hide him. But how shall we get him into the house without Bragshaw's knowledge?'

'Leave Master Bragshaw to me,' smiled Ned. 'I think I can keep him busy.'

'And I will guide Mun's friends to the house when they bring him,' said Elinor.

'Certainly not!' cried Philadelphia, coming to life again. 'Elinor, you will remain here.'

'But I have already been to the gate, Madam, and I have promised to help!'

'Let her go,' said Grandmother. 'I begin to have great confidence in Elinor. Our task must be to prepare for our patient.'

Philadelphia shook her head but she wiped her tears and followed Grandmother from the room. Ned turned to Elinor. 'We'll wait for

Bragshaw's visitor to go. Then, when you hear a bit of commotion from the kitchen, go straight to the stable. A horse will be ready. Take that for Master Edmund.'

Elinor stood at the parlour door. From there, she could see if anyone crossed the hall. They seemed to wait for a long time but, at last, Elinor turned and put her finger to her lips.

'Bragshaw's visitor is just leaving,' she whispered.

Suddenly, Ned's voice sounded loudly in the hall. 'Master Bragshaw! A message came for you.' Before he could continue, an appalling scream made their ears vibrate. Then another. Then two people, screaming horribly, from the kitchen.

Ned and Bragshaw ran into the kitchen and Elinor, followed by Tom and Bridget, ran too. Peering round the kitchen door, they saw Peg and Mistress Woodthorpe standing on benches. Both were screaming but Peg seemed quite demented. She was banging on the wall with a spoon.

'Stop it at once, you foolish creatures,' ordered Master Bragshaw. 'What is it?'

'Oh, Sir! Oh, Sir!' shouted Mistress Woodthorpe.

'This is disgraceful,' bawled Bragshaw. 'Stop this noise on the instant. What is wrong with you?'

He walked up to Peg and tried to pull the spoon away from her. She resisted, fell off the bench, and she and Bragshaw tumbled in a heap on the floor.

'You go,' grinned Tom. 'I'll keep watch.'

Elinor and Bridget ran to the stable and found the little horse ready. Even as far away as the field gate, they still heard a particularly piercing scream from the kitchen.

The scream had come from Bragshaw. As he lay on the floor, he had found himself nose to nose with an enormous grey rat. He and Peg leaped for the same bench.

'Catch it! Catch it!' he shouted, pushing Peg aside.

Ned ran round and round the room uttering cries of 'Vermin!', 'Oh dear!' and 'Heaven save us!' at intervals, but he was a poor rat catcher. When he crawled under the table, the rat seemed to be on top of it. He flapped his apron at it but that seemed to drive it towards Bragshaw. Finally the rat ran into a side room and Bragshaw threw himself across the kitchen to shut the door.

Bragshaw, so red in the face that he looked on the verge of an attack, sat down heavily and called for ale. 'Kill it,' he said, hoarsely.

'I'll fetch Pepper at once, Sir,' said Ned, 'but I was about to deliver a message. The boy from *The Civett Cat* was here. Some disturbance. Said you would want to know. Told him it was nonsense. "Master Bragshaw would not frequent an establishment such as *The Civett Cat*" I told him.'

Bragshaw was staring. 'A disturbance, you say?'

'Something to do with strangers in the neighbourhood.'

Bragshaw hesitated, then coughed and wiped his forehead. 'As I am master here at the present, I feel I should investigate. Get my horse ready and bring a cudgel. I may need protection.'

'I'll wager it's just the boy's nonsense,' insisted Ned but Bragshaw drove him out.

When they had gone, Peg took a small piece of bread and opened the door of the side room. She knelt down. 'Come along, my treasure,' she crooned and made little clicking noises. The bright-eyed rat took the bread from her and she picked it up. 'Were you frightened by all that noise, my pet? Did the horrid monster frighten you?'

Mistress Woodthorpe was putting the kitchen to rights. 'Take it out, Peg,' she said. 'I do not like it in the kitchen.'

'I could tell,' answered Peg, and they both started to laugh.

Tom ran down the path into the woods, smiling to himself. He couldn't wait to tell Bridget what had happened but when he reached the gate, he saw the girls kneeling by a figure on the ground.

'Oh, Tom!' said Bridget, her voice shaking, 'I'm glad you're here. It's Edmund. We'll have to lift him very carefully.'

Together, they struggled to get the young man to his feet, but they were appalled by his groans as they heaved him over the horse's back. With Elinor leading the animal and Tom and Bridget holding him on, they started back. He was dressed in much the same dirty clothing as the other young man but they were only too aware of the damp, dark stain spreading through the cloak over his shoulder. A wave of relief swept over Bridget as she saw Ned running towards them.

'Heaven preserve you, young master,' he said quietly and lifted Edmund off the beast and put him over his own strong shoulder. He carried him across the garden and into the house where Grandmother was waiting for them.

'My chamber,' she said, and Ned carried the now silent Edmund upstairs.

On the top step, Elinor sat down suddenly and started to cry. Tom and Bridget sat down with her and tried to comfort her. They wondered what they would do. They knew so much that the Bassingbourns did not. They had no antibiotics, no pain killers. Only hot water and herbs. Would it be enough? They sat in silence until the bedroom door opened and Philadelphia beckoned. All three slipped into the room.

Edmund, looking cleaner and tidier but horribly pale, lay propped on pillows in a bed hung with embroidered curtains. One arm was covered with a white cloth from shoulder to wrist. Grandmother sat beside him, holding a glass.

'My poor little Elinor!' said Edmund, holding out his uninjured arm. 'Do not look so frightened, I am not yet dead! Grandmother is taking good care of me.'

Elinor ran to her brother and started to cry again.

'Come, come!' said Grandmother, 'you have been so brave! The strongest spoke in the wheel of our fortune. Ned tells us you brought Edmund in alone.'

'It was a miracle!' said Edmund. 'But you must

be brave again, for my enemies are looking for me. I must prepare to move on.'

'You cannot,' said Philadelphia. 'You would not survive.'

'But I put you all in danger. A party of soldiers is already searching for me. They will undoubtedly come here.'

'You must stay for several days,' said Grandmother, quietly. 'If the wound is to heal, you must be still.'

Tom and Bridget stood immobile, just inside the door. It was as if they were watching television. Bridget was conscious of every object: the bright bed hangings, the pale sheets and bandages, and the young man's face which was the same colour as the creamy linen. It was not quite like television as she could smell the fruity cordial in the thick glass and the herby smell of the ointment. And she could feel fear. In this room, the Civil War was not about guns or politics. It was like it must be in any war, being afraid for people you love.

In the silence, they became aware of noises from outside the house. A voice called and there was the sound of running feet.

'Your father has returned,' said Grandmother, patting Edmund's hand. 'I think your fate is about to be decided, my child. Philadelphia, go and speak to your husband.'

Philadelphia hurried from the room. Still no one spoke. Elinor went to stand between Edmund and Grandmother. Then Philadelphia's quick steps were heard returning, accompanied by a heavier tread. They looked anxiously towards the door.

Tom and Bridget recognised the man framed in the doorway. John Bassingbourn, stern, un-smiling, dressed in black. But the wooden frame no longer belonged to the doorway. It was the frame of the portrait. They were back in the attic.

· 8 ·

The Gun

No one was happy that evening. Tom and Bridget felt as if they had been torn away from the most important thing in their lives. They desperately needed to know what was going to happen. Mr Wetherby was not very cheerful, either.

'I can't understand it,' he complained. 'I'm beginning to think someone destroyed all the papers from the seventeenth century. Where are they all?'

'But you have so much from all the other periods,' comforted Mum.

'That makes it worse in a way. Sorry, every-one,' he apologised. 'You see, the great thing about this house is that it is so complete – yet there's this big gap. Everyone thinks jewels and silver and so on are the real finds but, for an historian, it's the documents and details – they're the real treasures.'

'Perhaps you two should take a break tomor-row,' suggested Mum.

'No!' Tom and Bridget both spoke together and Mr Wetherby laughed.

'You're a shining example,' he said. 'I must pull myself together. Perhaps I'll go over to West-bridge House tomorrow. The Westbridge Family were related to the Bassingbourns. Might be some papers there.' He drummed his fingers on the table and frowned. 'Something happened in about the 1650s, I'm sure of it. You see, the house eventually passed to the younger son, Nathaniel. I suppose the elder son was killed in the Civil War. It's very frustrating, not knowing.'

Tom and Bridget looked at each other. Surely Edmund would not die? How would Elinor bear it? Yet he could be dying at this moment.

'Early night,' said Mum, looking at them and

Tom and Bridget were too worn out to resist. 'I just hope you will all have perked up by tomorrow.'

It rained heavily the next day. Mr Wetherby took a long time talking to the people working out in the barn. Then he hesitated about going over to Westbridge House but, at last, he and Mum left.

As soon as they left, Tom and Bridget went up to the attic. As they went into the room, they sensed a stillness. They waited, unsure of their next move. At last, Bridget could bear it no longer. She seized the rattle and put it in front of the portrait. They looked hopefully at the alcove but nothing happened. They tried the skillet again but everything remained unchanged. They tried the doll.

'Something is happening to prevent Elinor coming to us.' Bridget felt like crying. She wandered over to the window. The path through the woods was deserted. 'You remember the first day we came, Tom? I saw the path and the wall and that gate. I felt something then. That something dreadful was happening.'

Tom spoke behind her, 'I think this is what we

need.' Bridget turned. Tom was holding a pistol.

'Put it down, Tom,' she whispered. 'Guns are horrible.'

'I know.' Tom frowned. 'I don't want to play with it, or anything silly, but it's something to do with Elinor's time. We need it to take us to her.'

'When we put the rattle in front of the portrait, we were taken to the family. When it was the skillet, we ended up in the kitchen. What will happen when we put a gun there? It's too dangerous.'

'But we don't alter anything, Bridget,' he argued. 'The objects just make the link and it has to be the right link. Something dangerous *is* happening, now! Anyway, we've got to know what is happening to Edmund.' He looked at Bridget, pleading with her to agree.

'All right,' she said at last. 'I want to know, too.'

Tom went to the portrait and put the pistol down in front of it. Polished wood and chased silver. The pistol looked quite pretty until you thought what it could do. Bridget came across and stood close to Tom. The room seemed darker. The rain beat against the window. They both looked up at the portrait of John Bassingbourn and he looked steadily back, still unsmiling. Then, he spoke.

'How are you, Edmund?' He walked across to the bed.

Tom and Bridget found themselves back in Grandmother's room again, just inside the door, listening intently.

'I am much recovered, Sir,' Edmund answered, quietly.

'I had hoped you were safely in France.'

'I came back, Sir, and now I am a trouble to you all.'

'As sons are,' said Grandmother.

John Bassingbourn smiled slightly.

'I will go at once,' said Edmund, pulling himself up, 'if you would provide me with a horse.'

'You will stay, Edmund,' said his father firmly, 'until you are recovered. I will not abandon you though I regret our differences.'

'I shall never forget my duty to you, Sir.' Edmund spoke earnestly. 'But I believe his late Majesty was ordained by God to be our King and now I must remain loyal to his son.'

'And I believe your opinions are wrong. The

nature of government *must* change.' John Bassingbourn frowned and walked over to the window.

'Shall Mun be allowed to stay?' asked Elinor.

'For the moment. But Edmund, Ned tells me your part in the Royalist cause is known.'

'Bragshaw,' said Philadelphia, bitterly. 'Bragshaw betrayed him for money.'

'Then we must think of a place of safety. Can he travel a short distance, Madam?'

Old Mistress Bassingbourn shook her head. 'Impossible. But I have somewhere to hide him.' She turned to her daughter-in-law. 'You know that I have had some repairs made to my cupboard? The truth is that it did not need repairing. I have had some alterations made.'

She went to a door on the right of the fireplace and opened a cupboard, disguised by the panelling. It was a wardrobe, full of gowns and skirts. Grandmother moved some garments and showed them the floor. There was a trap door. Elinor darted forward and lifted it. Under the floorboards was a hiding place, very cramped, which might take one man. The only sign of its presence was the trap door. Old Mistress Bassingbourn looked straight at her son. John Bassingbourn looked sternly back.

'You will not be pleased,' she said. 'We are not of the same opinion on these matters.' She looked uncomfortable for a moment, then confessed. 'I felt I might have need of a priest's conveyance.

The poor creatures have been hunted like animals. I felt one day I might have to offer one shelter.'

'Madam!' protested John Bassingbourn, angrily, but Grandmother raised her hand.

'I give my word that no one shall be sheltered here except Edmund.'

Edmund was standing unsteadily, holding on to the bedpost. Philadelphia wrapped a cloak around him.

'Will you quarrel now?' she asked, sharply. 'Help Edmund into the hiding place.'

Then the yard was full of the sound of hooves, of heavy feet and shouting and there was a loud hammering on the front door.

'Go to the door, Sir,' said Grandmother, 'and admit our guests.'

Philadelphia closed the wardrobe door and sank into a chair while Elinor, Tom and Bridget huddled in a corner. The dream-like feeling came to Bridget again. She was part of the event and yet not part of it.

They listened to John Bassingbourn's calm tones. He was answered by a loud, arrogant voice. Soon, they began to hear several men moving around the house. Furniture was shifted. Then there were footsteps on the staircase. Someone crashed a hand down on the latch of the door and threw it open. A man stood in the doorway. He was holding a pistol.

· 9 ·

A Token of Friendship

Philadelphia sprang up as an officer and two men came into the room, followed by her husband. Through the open door, Tom and Bridget saw other soldiers continuing the search. John Bassingbourn took his wife's hand and forced her gently back into her chair.

'Be calm, my dear,' he murmured. 'This is Captain Eyre. He thinks the son of Charles Stuart is sheltering here. He has been absurdly misinformed.'

The Captain smiled, unpleasantly. 'You will forgive me, I am sure, if I carry out my duty and search this room.'

'This is my mother's chamber. Is it really necessary?'

'Your pardon, Madam.' The Captain bowed. He seemed to be mocking them. 'My men will be quick – but thorough.'

He stepped aside and the two soldiers came

forward and started tapping not only the panelled walls but the floor, too. They seemed experienced. Tom breathed in sharply. He realised what they were doing. As soon as they reached the cupboard concealed by the panelling, it would sound hollow. They would hear the difference immediately. He watched, breathing fast, as the men carefully circled the room. Bridget was white and Elinor gripped a chair, her eyes wide open. One of the soldiers reached the wall with the cupboard in it and began, methodically, to tap his way towards it.

Suddenly, Philadelphia rose to her feet. She was no longer the softly-spoken gentlewoman. She was blazingly angry.

'You are a disgrace, Sir! How dare you disturb us! Come, search everywhere. I insist! Look in the clothes closet. Perhaps we have a prince among the petticoats!' She threw open the cupboard door. 'Search the bed hangings!' She jerked back the curtain and pulled at the coverlet. 'Search the table drawer!' She wrenched the tiny drawer out of the little oak table. 'Are good people to be treated in this shameful way by ruffians like yourself?'

All eyes were on Captain Eyre. Tom watched, fascinated, as he turned a strange, dull red. Like beetroot with the earth still on, he thought. Bridget thought she might be sick. The man had enjoyed it when he thought they were afraid. Now he was furious. 'I shall search, Madam, never fear. I shall search every corner of this house, even the smallest space.' He spoke quietly in a kind of hiss. He strode up to the cupboard and with a vicious sweep of the hand which held the gun, knocked all the clothing to the floor, tearing silk and lace.

Bridget and Tom stared at each other, mouths open. The Captain himself had concealed the trap door!

Beside himself with anger, he tore down the bed hangings. 'You women, stay where you are. You, Sir! You come with me. We will search this house, step by step.'

He swept out of the room, the two soldiers hustling John Bassingbourn after him. Elinor ran to her mother who clutched her. They were both shaking. Old Mistress Bassingbourn came over to them and patted them, too agitated herself to do anything except murmur, 'Well done, my dear, well done!'

They stayed as they were for an age. They heard footsteps running, loud knocking and angry shouts, even a scream from the kitchen. The Captain was venting his anger.

'How clever she is,' thought Bridget, looking at Philadelphia in some surprise. 'She has made him angry and it has stopped him from being careful.'

There was a noise from the road. They heard the clatter of many horses' hooves and many men's feet. There was more shouting, this time from outside and Elinor ran to the window.

'It's the rest of the troop. They are calling for the Captain.'

Tom moved over to look through the little panes. Something had happened. A man on horseback waved impatiently and Captain Eyre called his men. In a few moments, the house was empty. It was over. John Bassingbourn stood grasping his own gate, looking after the disappearing soldiers and then turned and slowly walked back down the path. Tom turned round to find everyone in the room was crying, including himself!

They opened the hiding place and helped Edmund out.

Elinor was extremely indignant about the state of her own little room at the turn of the stairs. The door was open and the trunk was turned upside down. Bridget and Tom helped her to tidy up.

'Now Father knows what a traitor Bragshaw is, he will never allow him to return. That is a great mercy,' said Elinor, with satisfaction.

'What will happen to Edmund?' asked Tom.

'My father will try and send him safely to France, I am sure.'

'I hope he makes it,' said Tom, fervently. 'I wish him luck.'

'I wish we could know,' said Bridget, wistfully. 'I want to know what happens to you, too, Elinor. I'm afraid we might not find out.'

'How so?' asked Elinor.

'Well . . .' Bridget hesitated. 'You understand that we are not from your time, don't you? In our time, we don't know anything about your family. There are not many papers or records so you will be lost in time.'

'No,' said Elinor, 'I do not choose to be lost in time. I shall leave you a sign and some token of my friendship.' She jumped up. 'Come,' she called, bossily, 'we must find Pepper and tell him his enemy is defeated!'

Tom smiled as she ran out. 'She won't be able to leave us a sign. You can't leave things around for hundreds of years. Things get moved. They get lost.'

'Come. Follow!' Her imperious little voice floated back to them.

'Better follow the boss,' said Tom.

They ran down the stairs and tried to catch Pepper as he ran round and round the hall, barking. He darted back up the stairs and they ran after him, laughing and breathless. He charged right up to the top, then stopped, quite suddenly. They saw him crouch low and he began to whine. As they arrived at the door, its colour darkened and the latch began to blur.

'Quickly,' screamed Elinor, 'the way is closing.'

Tom understood. He grabbed Bridget and threw himself forward, pulling her with him into the attic. The door was now very narrow and, in a moment, it had gone. They stood on the other side, panting.

'What happened?' gasped Bridget.

'It began to close when we were on the stairs.'

Bridget's eyelids prickled. 'Is it over, Tom? Has she really gone?' The attic seemed lonely and empty. 'Let's go into the garden. I don't want to be in here now.'

They walked quietly downstairs and out of the front door. It was still raining a little but the sun was trying to shine. They walked round the side of the house and went into the garden. Tom looked up at the windows.

'Do you remember when we saw the little light in the window that night?'

Bridget followed his gaze. Bridget saw a tiny window half hidden by the buttress. 'Tom!' she said, 'I think that's the window to Elinor's little room on the staircase. Do you think we can get to it from the hall? Where the bottom of the stairs would have been?'

They dashed round the side of the house and back through the front door. They crossed the hall and found a door where the foot of the back stairs had been. Wrenching it open, they found buckets and brooms. They peered inside and inspected the back wall.

'Look at the floor,' said Bridget, 'They're the same flagstones. The staircase is here.'

'Great heavens!' said Mr Wetherby's voice. 'You're not going to take on the cleaning as well, are you?'

Tom stumbled out of the cupboard, waving a mop. 'It's a secret room, Mr Wetherby! You must believe us! It's Elinor's room.'

Mr Wetherby made them explain calmly. They had to show him the window, then he came and tapped the back of the cupboard. 'Well, it *is* just a partition,' he admitted, but he would not commit himself until he had fetched the house plans. 'There certainly is something here. I thought it was part of a chimney breast but it could be a disused staircase.' He smiled at them. 'After all, you don't have windows for nothing. I'll get a drill from the barn and just make a tiny hole.'

A shower of plaster resulted in a larger hole than he had really intended and once Mr Wetherby saw the staircase, there was no holding him. He enlarged the hole and squeezed through. They heard his feet on the staircase. A moment later, his plaster-covered head came back through the hole.

'You're right,' he beamed. 'There is a room up here. Come and see.'

Elinor's room was much as they had last seen it. A stool and a large chest had been added but the little trunk was there and the table with a cherub's head handle on its drawer. Bridget's heart turned over when Mr Wetherby opened the drawer and found a tinder box. Bridget and Tom smiled at each other.

A little later, down in the hall, everyone gathered round as Mr Wetherby opened the chest. It was full of papers. He began to look at them, laying them out carefully.

'What luck,' he said, softly. 'What wonderful luck! Who needs wills when you can have all this?'

'Is this what you were looking for?' asked Mum.

'More than that. A full house inventory and all kinds of everyday papers – the sort that usually get thrown away. Look: bills, notes for trades-men, farm accounts, even plans for the garden. This is a treasure chest.' They had never seen a man so happy.

'What about this?' Mum had picked up a book and was leafing through it, smiling. 'It's a recipe book for medicines. All sorts of herbal concoctions.'

Tom and Bridget peered over her shoulder and realised they were probably looking at Grand-mother's handwriting. *'For a despratt cold . . .'* it said.

'Ah!' said Mr Wetherby. 'Remember I told you I'd found one mysterious letter from Edmund Bassingbourn? Here are the rest of them.' He held up a large packet of letters, tied together with ribbon. 'Must have a look at these.'

'Please,' begged Bridget, 'find out where he was when he wrote them. Where are they from?'

Mr Wetherby looked at her curiously but he undid the packet. 'France,' he said at last. 'This is quite fascinating. He seems to have escaped to France sometime after the battle of Worcester. Well, that's possible. Charles himself was hidden in a house near here. These seem to be addressed to his younger sister, Elinor.'

'And here she is,' said Mum's voice. 'Isn't this absolutely delightful?'

She was holding a miniature painting. She passed it to Mr Wetherby. Over his shoulder, Bridget and Tom saw Elinor's happy face, a little older but just as lively.

'It's even signed,' he said, sighing contentedly. On the back was written *'Elinor Bassingbourn. This is my Sign to those I have never Forgotten. A Token of Friendship.'*

'She kept her promise,' said Bridget, quietly.

'Of course, she did,' answered Tom. 'She was that kind of ghost.'

'What?' asked Mum. 'What did you say?'

'I said she was that kind of girl,' grinned Tom.

Further Reading

Now that you have read **A Ghost-Light in the Attic**, you might like to read some other books about life in Stuart times. You might like to read other novels or general information books. Here is a selection of the books available.

Fiction

Monica Dickens	**The Great Fire**, *Mammoth, Reed Books (1993)*
Berlie Doherty	**Children of Winter**, *Mammoth, Reed Books (1994)*
Linda Kempton	**The Naming of William Rutherford**, *Mammoth, Reed Books (1994)*
Geoffrey Trease	**Fire on the Wind**, *Pan Macmillan Children's Books, Macmillan (1994)*

Non-fiction

Tessa Hosking	**The Tudors and Stuarts**, *(in the* **Look into the Past** *series), Wayland Books (1995)*
Rhoda Nottridge	**The Gunpowder Plot**, *Wayland Books (1993)*
Rhoda Nottridge	**Plague and Fire**, *Wayland Books (1993)*
Philip Sauvain	**Tudors and Stuarts**, *(in the* **Family Life** *series), Wayland Books (1995)*
Rachel Wright	**Stuarts**, *(in the* **Craft Topics** *series), Watts Books (1993)*